The Porcelain Pepper Pot

WRITTEN AND ILLUSTRATED BY ALAIN VAËS

BOSTON LITTLE, BROWN AND COMPANY TORONTO

FIRST EDITION

Library of Congress Cataloging in Publication Data

Vaës, Alain.
  The porcelain pepper pot.

  Summary: A pepper pot, left behind by picnickers in the French countryside, seeks his fortune, and finds it in a beautiful farmhouse saltcellar.
  [1. Tableware — Fiction. 2. Farm life — Fiction]
I. Title.
PZ7.V18Po   [E]   82-15303
ISBN 0-316-89503-2   AACR2
ISBN 0-316-89502-4 (pbk.)

AHS

Published simultaneously in Canada by Little, Brown & Company (Canada) Limited

PRINTED IN THE UNITED STATES OF AMERICA

To *Gwenaëlle*

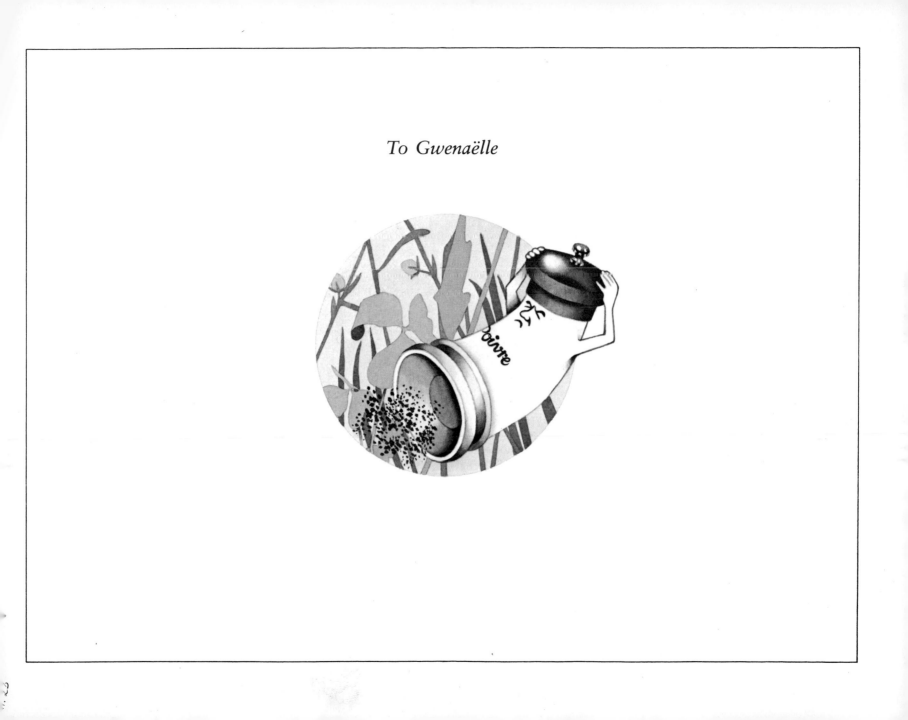

In France one day not so long ago a little porcelain pepper pot was forgotten by a group of picnickers after a lunch in the country.

He decided to try to find his way to a friendly house where he might be of use, so he struck out on his own and wandered through fields and forests.

The ways of country creatures were new to him. He passed some mice who were building a house. "Hello," he said, but they were so busy that they didn't bother to return his greeting.

8

Next, he had to defend himself from an angry raccoon who didn't want the pepper pot in his part of the meadow.

At last he came to a farm. "This place looks as if it might make a fine home," he thought.

The chickens in the barnyard, however, did not welcome him. "Out of here, you strange-looking creature," they clucked. The rooster, who was a bully, tried to give the pepper pot a peck and send him on his way.

The pepper pot made short work of them.

Leaving the farmyard, he cautiously approached the house and peered in.

On the mantel above the stove was the loveliest salt cellar he had ever seen. The pepper pot fell in love at once. He climbed up to her and told her of his feelings.

She blushed prettily and took his arm. However, a bad-tempered pepper mill who lived in the kitchen also loved the salt cellar.

"Leave her alone!" he bellowed. "If you don't get out of here at once, I will thrash you."

He didn't expect the porcelain pepper pot to beat him
so easily.

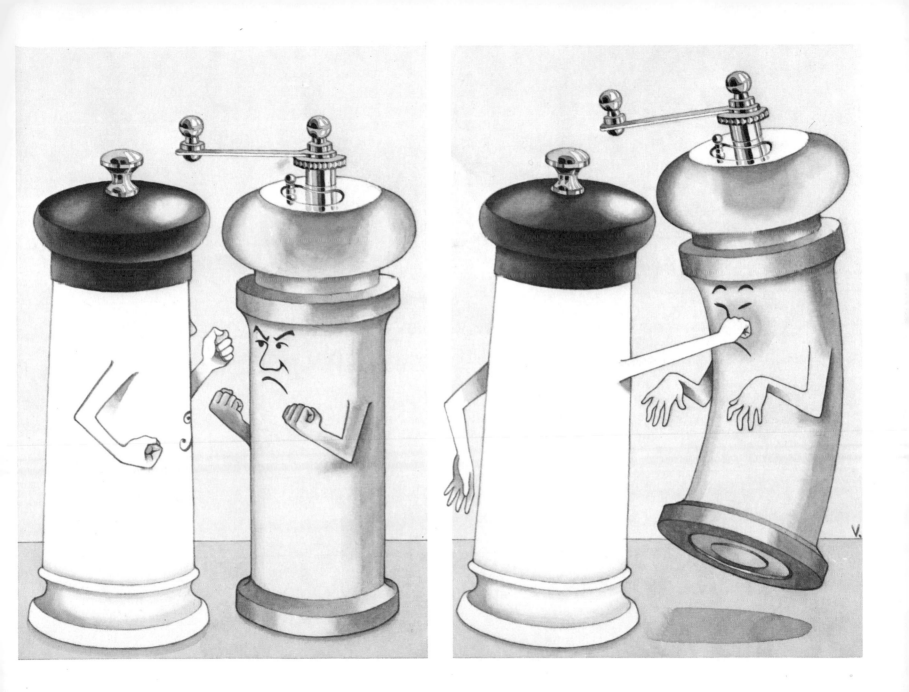

The other pots in the kitchen cheered the outcome. "Long life to the victor!" they cried. "Let us celebrate."

That very night the little porcelain pepper pot wed his own true love.

They soon had a family, and surrounded by their children they lived a long and happy life together.

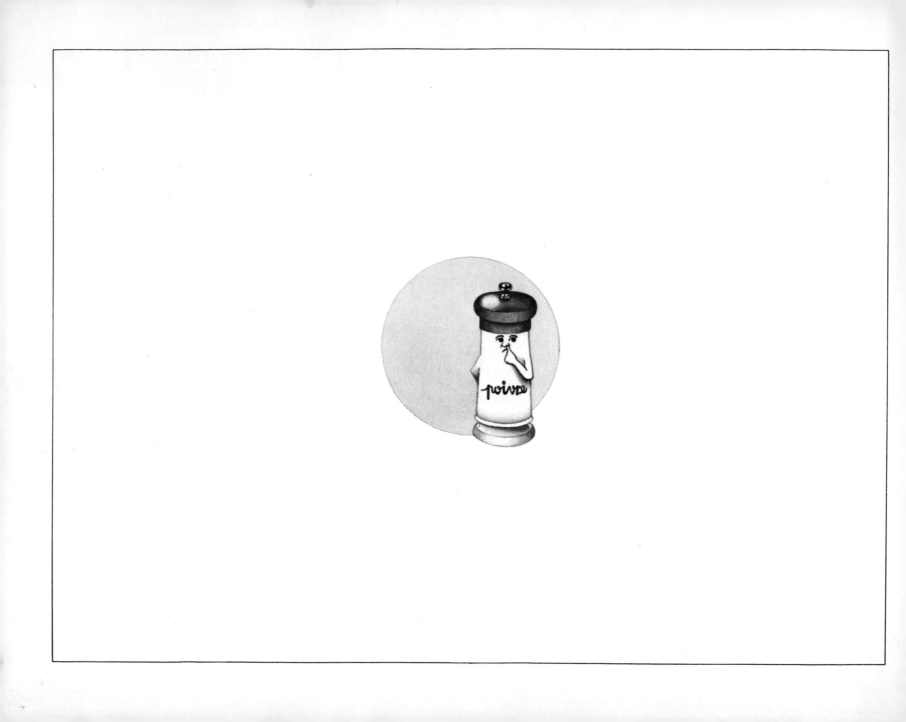